D0919311

Amy Price for President!

Charley Pickle

An imprint of Enslow Publishing

Amy Price for President!

Maci Masaki Makes her Mark

What's the Matter with Jayden Jackson??

Eli Michaels, Rule Breaker

Please visit our website, www.west44books.com. For a free color catalog of all our high-quality books, call toll free 1-800-542-2595 or fax 1-877-542-2596.

Cataloging-in-Publication Data

Names: Pickle, Charley.
Title: Amy Price for president! / Charley Pickle.
Description: New York : West 44, 2019. | Series: We the weirdos
Identifiers: ISBN 9781538382035 (pbk.) | ISBN 9781538382042 (library bound) | ISBN 9781538383025 (ebook)
Subjects: LCSH: Friendship--Juvenile fiction. | Schools--Juvenile fiction. | School elections--Juvenile fiction. | Self-confidence in children--Juvenile fiction.
Classification: LCC PZ7.P535 Am 2019 | DDC [E]--dc23

First Edition
Published in 2019 by
Enslow Publishing
111 East 14th Street, Suite 349
New York, NY 10003

Editor: Theresa Emminizer
Designer: Sam DeMartin

Photo credits: cover, front matter (Amy Price) Digital Vision/Photodisc/Getty Images; cover, front matter (peace, heart, star) gst/Shutterstock.com; cover (vote) Natasha Pankina/Shutterstock.com; cover (sneaker) Visual Generation/Shutterstock.com; front matter (Maci Masaki) Plattform/Getty Images; front matter (Jayden Jackson) Arthur Dries/The Image Bank/Getty Images; front matter (Eli Michaels) Juan monino/E+/Getty Images; front matter (Maci Masaki signature) Very_Very/Shutterstock.com; p. 2 (pantsuit) AuraArt/Shutterstock.com; p. 9 (robot) grzhmelek/Shutterstock.com; p. 14 (drain) olllikeballoon/Shutterstock.com; p. 16 (sneakers) Ole Lookole/Shutterstock.com; p. 21 (panther) Rachaya Yodsuwan/Shutterstock.com; pp. 22 (squirrel), 26 (flag) Ohn Mar/Shutterstock.com; p. 22 (crown) LHF Graphics/Shutterstock.com; p. 23 (fish tank) Julia Khimich/Shutterstock.com; p. 33 (rocket) Padma Sanjaya/Shutterstock.com; p. 26 (ice cream) primiaou/Shutterstock.com; back matter (skulls) zizi_mentos/Shutterstock.com; back matter (bomb) dicogm/Shutterstock.com.

Printed in the United States of America

CPSIA compliance information: Batch #CS18W44: For further information contact Enslow Publishing LLC, New York, New York at 1-800-542-2595.

WE THE
WEIRDOS

Amy Price

Clubs and Activities:
Class President

Most Likely to Be
President of the
United States

Quote: "When life
hands you a lemon,
take the lemon and
run with it!"

Amy Price

Jayden Jackson

Clubs and Activities:
–

Most Likely to
Win a Fight

Quote: "Get out of
my face, dude."

JAYDEN JACKSON

ELI MICHAELS

Clubs and Activities: choir, cooking club, Volunteer club

Most Likely to Cheer You Up

Quote: "Do the right thing, and the sun will always shine your way!"

Maci Masaki

Clubs and Activities: Art Club

Most Likely to Become a Famous Artist

Quote: "I wish life were in watercolor."

weirdo: a strange or unique person who is often not accepted by a larger group

CHAPTER ONE
Talking Is Trouble

I am running to Public School 71. And I am wearing a red pantsuit. It's my mom's pantsuit. She wore it when she was elected president of our block club.

I am wearing it so I do not have to speak when I get to P.S. 71. I do not want to speak. I have a stutter. A bad stutter. The suit will speak for me.

As I run, this is what I think:

They will like you, Amy. They will think you are funny. Because this suit is funny! A kid in a suit. That's funny. And cool. Super retro. Those P.S. 71 kids will beg you to be their friend.

The red suit is hard to run in. But, I am not afraid of doing hard things.

Friends! New friends! Oh man. They are going to be city kids. Real city kids. Not like the kids at my old school. Mosaic Elementary.

I am running to the subway station. I run past the flower shop. The air smells like lilies.

Usain Bolt imagines each race before he runs it. And he's the fastest person in the world. So I imagine my first day of middle school.

The other sixth graders will laugh, "OMG! Your suit is red! Power red? Girl, you're so funny! You should run for president! I'll vote for you."

I will nod. I will smile. I already know when the P.S. 71 election is. Four weeks from today.

The sixth graders will open the door for me. They'll say, "Wow. You are way funnier than any other kid at this school!"

I'll laugh, modestly.

Then they'll see my neon green track shoes. They'll say, "No way, Amy! Can you get any cooler?"

I will shake my head, like, "No. I don't think I can get any cooler!"

They will laugh more. "Wow, the new kid is, like, really funny."

They will open the doors to their school. They'll invite me to their lunch table. We will eat peanut butter sandwiches. We will make sounds with our armpits. I will tell all my favorite corny jokes. They will laugh so hard that milk will spill out of their noses.

And when I talk, it will be clear. I will speak as clearly as former president Barack Obama. If I hear someone else stutter, I will say, "Glad that's not me!"

Outside the subway stop, a man calls, "Hot coffee! One buck! Get your hot coffee, ladies and gentleman! Only one dollar!"

He smiles at my red suit. He is missing a front tooth. I smile, too.

I sprint to P.S. 71. The man calls out, "Watch out world! That girl is on fire!"

I feel the wind rush through my hair. I run past the Clinton Street Grocery. Past the Baptist church. And into the courtyard of Public School 71.

I cannot wait to hear these sixth graders laugh at my joke. The red suit is super funny.

I walk past a fountain without water. In the center of the fountain is a panther statue. The panther is made out of iron. It looks angry.

CHAPTER TWO
Joke's on Me

At the fountain, my red pantsuit is damp with sweat. Ninety-six kids walk past the fountain. No one looks me in the eye.

The P.S. 71 sixth graders look different than the kids at Mosaic. Mosaic students wore whatever clothes they wanted. Mosaic students wore shirts with islands on them. They wore skirts with trees on them. They wore hats with taxis on them. They wore feathers in their hair. Mosaic students sat on yoga balls. They danced to ocean songs.

None of the P.S. 71 kids have stickers

on their face. Or green lipstick. Or rabbit-ear hairbands. I feel strange. I feel out of place. They look like an army unit that I am not in. A cool army unit.

P.S. 71 kids wear uniforms. Neat khaki pants. Blue collared shirts with tiny yellow panthers on the pocket. Their hair is pulled up tightly behind their heads. Girls wear round gold earrings. Some earrings hold the letters of their names.

I guess I didn't get the memo about everything at P.S. 71. I'm starting a couple of weeks late. And Jim, the counselor at Mosaic, said he'd take care of everything. But then he forgot to send my grades. I realize now he also forgot to tell my parents about the uniforms. My mom said Jim probably didn't know how to use a computer. He was probably too busy studying fish with the students. That made my dad laugh. My mom never liked Mosaic as much as I did. That's why I go here now. It's also a public school. Mosaic cost too much.

The P.S. 71 sixth graders talk to each other on the school steps. No one laughs at my red business suit.

Instead, a kid scrunches her face and says, "Uh…weird!" Then she bolts up the steps away from me.

Suddenly, a kid with beautiful, thick hair notices me.

He looks at his phone and answers it. "Hello?"

He looks at me. He listens to his phone for two seconds. Then he says, "Sure!"

He holds the phone to me. "It's for you."

Who is calling me? Maybe he's friends with one of my old friends? Lucia?

I try to tell my brain to say something normal like, "Really?" But instead, I enter into scared silence.

The kid's eyes widen and he shouts, "It's my

grandmother. She wants her clothes back!"

I try to speak, but I can't. I try to say, *That's a horrible joke.*

But all I say is, "You! You! Your! You're." Until I am exhausted.

Here's the deal: I've had a speech therapist since third grade. When she told me and my parents that I had a stutter, she said, "The label of your disability doesn't matter. Just take a deep breath in and try again. It's okay to repeat things. Most people are kind."

She was wrong.

"That's n-n-not…that's so not funny!" I say.

I feel the muscles of my face twitch. I think, *Take a breath, Amy. Take one breath.* But I can't. I can't calm down. My heartbeat feels like a drum.

A sixth grader shouts, "Burn!" And then he high fives the boy who pranked me. He mocks me, saying, "Up Top, Dig-dig-dig-by!!"

A bunch of kids laugh when this kid fake-stutters.

"C-c-c-cool j-j-joke," I say.

I hear other kids say:

"Why is she talking like that?"

"Is she a robot?"

"Is she from another planet?"

I look down at my red pantsuit. I can't see their faces. All I hear is their voices. Mean, cruel voices.

"New kid is a weirdo."

Some kid pretends to be a robot. "Alert! Alert! Weirdo alert. Threat level high."

Digby laughs and points at me. His hair is no longer beautiful. He looks like a scorpion fish.

We learned a lot about fish at Mosaic. When my teacher put a photo of a scorpion fish on the board, he said,

"This fish is poisonous. It kills its prey with a stinger."

Digby's hair looks like a scorpion fish stinger.

I stutter, "You, you, you guys are the weird-d-d ones."

Digby laughs, "Really? You might want to check yourself on that one, Grammy!"

Digby's friend walks up to him. "Yo! Class, Digs." She is laughing. They both stare at me.

When I stare back, the friend says, "What? What's *your* problem?"

I try to yell something, but nothing comes out. The words pile up inside a net in my brain. Painful silence.

Then, Digby does something weird. He smiles a fake smile at me and says, "Take it easy, Grammy! I'm just *joking* with you."

"Okay," I say, confused.

They both laugh and walk up the steps of their school. Their school. Definitely not my school.

They. They have friends. They have jokes. They have uniforms.

I am a sweaty girl in a red pantsuit. No one got my joke. No one thinks I'm hilarious. And I don't have their stupid uniform because of stupid Jim and his stupid fish. Now I have to wear this red suit the entire day.

Digby and all the other kids do not notice my face. They do not see that it is tight with pain. And Digby just keeps laughing. And the laughter keeps stinging me.

I know then he is a bad fish.

CHAPTER THREE
In the Drain

For a new kid at a new school, September is the loneliest month.

And the problem is that I want to be their president. I want P.S. 71 to be as easy as Mosaic. If this were Mosaic, I would have no problem being president.

Like my mom.

My mom, the block club president. She gives speeches. She organizes protests. She even asked the city to make the sidewalks wheelchair friendly. She tells our neighbors how to make gardens in their backyards. She tells them how to contact the governor. She is amazing. My mom is a leader. When she speaks, every single person listens.

I'm wearing her red suit. I thought it would make me as powerful as her.

Last night before bed, I thought, *Maybe on my first day of this new school, my stutter will disappear. Maybe everything will get easier for me.*

This was wrong. It was a dream. It was a lie I told to myself.

I hear a loud ding of the bell. At Mosaic there were no bells. The sound of this bell is alarming.

All of the kids who had been laughing at me and calling me a weirdo rush into the school. Their walking turns to running. The cement steps shake with their force.

I notice that someone smells like a wet sheep. I realize that person is me.

I am alone on the steps. I look out at the

empty courtyard of Public School 71. I look at the fountain. I look at the panther statue.

I turn and run to the fountain.

The water is turned off, but there is a drain opening. Its cover is loose. I open it. And climb in.

I fit perfectly. It is dark and quiet.

This is perfect! I will never have to go into the school. I can tell my parents I'm going to school, but really just go to the drain each day. Problem solved.

CHAPTER FOUR
Sunshine

I am not going into this horrible school. The drain is amazing. I love it. There is a pipe to my left. I put my ear to it. I can hear the sound of water dripping.

It's so relaxing. Like the "Sounds of Nature" music at Mosaic.

But then, I hear someone singing: "You are my sunshine, my only sunshine." The singer has a calm, strong, Gospel-singer voice. It's nice to sit in the drain and listen.

Suddenly, I hear feet step onto the fountain. I look up. I see a pair of red Jordans.

And then the singing stops. A face peers into the drain.

"Hey, why are you in there?"

I freeze.

"You hurt?" he asks.

I'm silent.

"Say something!"

"N-n-n-no," I whisper.

He reaches out his hand. "Come out then. This is a crazy place to take a nap!"

"I wasn't nap-nap—"

I think: *He's going to make fun of me for my stutter. Run!*

But the singer doesn't laugh at me. He just waits until I finish stuttering. He is patient.

Then he asks, "So, who are you?"

"I'm a n-n-new student. I'm Amy P-p-rice."

"Cool!" He helps me stand up. He brushes the dirt off my arms. "Welcome to the finest public school in the city!"

"Thanks," I say. I think he's mistaken.

"Amy Price," he says. "The price is right! Just messing with you!" He laughs.

He has a nice smile. His nice smile makes me smile, too. This makes my face feel relaxed. Like I can breathe again.

"Well, I'm Eli Michaels, and I do not have scoliosis! I had to get the test this morning at the doctor's office. My spine is egg-cellent. So that's super good. I'm just a little late to class."

I laugh. Eli seems cozy. Like a family member. He is like tomato soup on a rainy day.

I get out of the drain. We walk up the steps of P.S. 71.

I open the doors of the school and a rush of smells hits me. Body spray, french fries, and mint gum. "Whoa!" I say.

"You'll get used to the smell of this school. It's not like any place in the world!"

That's definitely true, I think.

The bell rings. Eli freaks. "That's the second period bell! You got a schedule, Price Is Right? We cannot be late!"

I do have a schedule, and it says I need to be in Science at 8:28 a.m. That's in one minute.

"Got to go, Eli. Thank you!"

"Find me at lunch!" he calls out. Then Eli disappears into the wild sea of sixth graders.

CHAPTER FIVE
Gross!

Science is on the third floor. I sprint up the steps.

The bell rings. I am in the room. I just don't have a seat.

I see ten tables. There is an empty seat next to a kid who has headphones on. When he sees me, he shakes his head. "Taken."

I look around the room for another spot. There isn't one.

"I h-h-have to sit here."

He looks at me, angry and annoyed. "Fine. But don't talk, okay?"

"I hate t-t-talking!" I stutter.

He nods. Then goes super quiet.

A teacher with a very red, runny nose comes up to the front of the room. My schedule says she's Ms. Shelby. "Good morning. Let's jump right in to learning today. First, we'll study apex predators!"

She claps her hands together. A tissue falls out of her blouse.

"So, what's the deal with apex predators?"

Then, she sneezes.

No one says *Bless you*.

Ms. Shelby pulls another tissue out of her pocket. She wipes her nose. She puts it back into her pocket.

Digby yells out, "GROSS!"

A lot of kids laugh.

Ms. Shelby glares at Digby.

Digby shuts up. The kids stop laughing.

"As I was saying, an apex predator is on the top of the food chain. It is the most powerful animal. Top dog. It has no predator. For example, a panther is an apex predator. A panther hunts the forest with the motto..." She sneezes again.

Digby starts to say "Gross!" until Ms. Shelby looks right at him.

She says, "I eat the weak!"

We are all silent. She laughs.

"Tough crowd!" she says.

I smile. She is funny.

"Well, here's the thing. Not all big animals are apex predators. Say a panther lived with toxic squirrels. The squirrels would be the apex predator. The environment, the ecosystem, decides the apex predators."

The class quiets.

"Please write down questions and notes."

I write the following:

1. Is Digby an apex predator? Yes. He is a panther.

2. Am I an apex predator? No. Not in the ecosystem of P.S. 71.

3. Can I become one? Can I become a panther?

4. Maybe.

5. Yes?

6. Yes, I CAN.

CHAPTER SIX
The Weirdo Table

After Science, I go to two other classes. Then I look at my schedule. Sixth graders have first lunch at 11:00 a.m. Which is now!

When I enter the cafeteria, I don't know where to sit. The cafeteria has one fish tank in the corner. There are only four lonely fish in the tank. I see a bright yellow

sign on the wall. It says, “Class Elections October 25th. If you wish to be considered, tell the main office your name by September 28th.” That’s tomorrow!

I see a group of three girls and one boy eating their lunch. I walk up near them. They are reading each other their jokes from their string cheese wrappers.

“What’s black and white and red all over?” one girl asks.

“I’ve heard this like a million times! A newspaper!” someone replies.

“Nope, a panda in a cherry costume!” the girl says. “Gotcha!”

I laugh loudly. “Good one!” I make a giant thumbs-up in the air.

Their laughter stops.

“C-c-can, I sit sit sit here?” I ask.

“Um…no,” the joke girl says.

“We’re not being mean,” the boy says.

"We're just, like, already friends with each other."

"Oh. Cool!" I smile. It's fake. My face gets hot. *Yeah, obviously you're already friends. But at some point, you weren't already friends. And I need friends. So lame!*

I walk to another table. As I walk over, the kids scoot together. I can't sit down.

Wow, I think. *Really nice kids here at P.S. 71. Really good social skills, you guys. I'm sure you will all be president of…NOTHING!*

Then I hear someone singing over all the cafeteria noises.

I look over at the farthest end of the cafeteria. There is one sad-looking table. It has a brown top. It looks like fake wood. There are benches on either side. It is big enough for six people. It is near the lonely fish tank. There's only one boy sitting alone.

Eli Michaels.

As I walk over, I hear him humming to

his juice box. I think it's that song from that old musical *Oklahoma*.

He stops when he sees me. He smiles wide. "Hi, Amy Price! How are you?"

"H-h-hi, Eli. Can I s-s-sit here?" I feel pathetic.

"Yes, you can…nada! O Canada!" Eli is clearly delighted. He is also very patriotic. Maybe he is from Canada.

"Welcome to the Weirdo Table!" Eli sings in an opera singer's voice.

"Weirdo Table?" I ask.

"Yep," he nods. "My name is Eli, and I am a total weirdo." He smiles super huge. He is proud of this joke.

"Why a weirdo?"

"I don't really know. But I know that I am one!"

I shake my head. "Who said that?"

He sighs. "Digby Praxton. He's a bully. He's what my mom—she's a pastor—would call 'someone who needs a little help from above.'"

I nod. Digby Praxton. I think:

He's so mean. Can a panther be a panther without being mean?

I sit next to Eli.

Suddenly, I see a hand on the bench. It disappears under the table.

Am I seeing things? I think: *I am already more of a weirdo than before.*

Eli doesn't notice the hand. Instead, he opens his lunch and whispers, "I have blueberry pie!"

"I have yo-yo-yogurt!" I blush because my stutter is really annoying.

Quickly, I put the tube of yogurt in my mouth and pretend to play it like a wooden flute. I move my fingers and make jazzy flute noises.

Eli laughs really hard. "You are seriously hilarious, Amy Price!"

My shoulders drop. I giggle.

Eli and I talk and giggle and talk and giggle the entire lunch period.

I need some more information about the elections at P.S. 71. So, I ask him who's running.

He says, "Digby. And, he will definitely win. If you put your name in, know that you are probably not going to win. He's getting everyone to vote for him by saying he'll get more desserts in the cafeteria."

"But!" Eli says, raising his finger like a conductor. "It would be a cool if you ran anyway. You'll make a speech in the auditorium!"

My stomach drops.

"In front of everyone!" Eli adds.

I have to make a speech in front of everyone? The whole school?

Eli chants, "Amy Price! The Price is Right!

Amy Price!"

There is no way I can make a speech. I feel like I might be sick.

Eli starts singing again. "You are my sunshine! My only sunshine! And if you run for pres-i-dent, I will vote for you!"

I'm still scared. But I can't help but smile at Eli. I smile like Usain Bolt when he wins a race.

Eli makes me remember what happiness feels like.

But then, I scream.

Something grabbed my ankle.

CHAPTER SEVEN
Under the Weirdo Table

"Something grabbed me!" I yell. I nearly jump out of my seat.

"Dude, relax," a voice says, next to me. It's the angry kid from Science. I didn't even see him sit down. This table gets weirder by the minute.

The angry kid has gray Jordans on. And a gray hoodie. And a gray hat that says LA LAKERS on it.

"You're not supposed to wear hats in school, Jayden," Eli says.

The angry kid is named Jayden.

Jayden takes off his Lakers hat. "*Relax.*"

"Lakers, not Knicks?" I ask Jayden.

"My dad plays for the Lakers," Jayden says. He holds his hat tight in his hands.

"Whoa!" Eli says.

Jayden doesn't make eye contact with me when he says his dad plays for the Lakers. I want to know why. Instead, I think, *What grabbed my ankle? P.S. 71 is a wild place.*

I look under the table. There is a girl sitting on the ground. She is drawing in a notebook. A seahorse with huge eyes.

"Is that m-m-manga?" I ask.

She closes her eyes.

"I can still s-s-see you," I say.

She keeps her eyes closed and shakes her head, no.

"Um, okay," I say. I sit back up and ask Eli, "You know, there's s-s-omeone under the table?"

"Yeah!" Eli smiles. "That's Maci!"

Eli shifts his body on the bench. He says, "You aren't allowed to sit under the table, Maci."

Eli really likes rules. He is a little annoying. But an annoying friend is better than no friend. Joe the counselor told me that.

Eli must read my thoughts. He starts humming a Christmas song. "Our church is putting on a Christmas musical. And I need to practice. Even if it's really early."

I nod, "You're really a g-g-good singer. You don't seem nervous singing in front of people."

Eli smiles.

"Why do you want to be president if you have a stutter?" Eli asks.

I blush. I had lied to myself. I thought he hadn't noticed my stutter. He never joked about it.

"Because then people will l-l-listen to me," I say.

When I say this, I feel like crying.

Eli nods. The bell rings. We recycle our paper bags and throw the rest into the garbage.

Eli grabs my arm. He asks, "Want to sing as we walk to class?"

This sounds like a terrible idea. But I nod. Maybe I can be as confident a weirdo as Eli.

Eli grabs my hand. "*You are my sunshine, my only sunshine*," Eli sings sweetly, as if singing to me.

I blush. I sing the lyrics back to him very quietly. We keep singing down the hall.

When we get to our lockers, Eli says, "You don't stutter when you sing."

It's true. I don't. This makes me feel brave.

I sprint to the main office.

I'm very quiet when I run. No teachers yell at me.

"How can I help you, young lady?" says the main office person. She has a rocket ship pin on her blouse. And really cool pink glasses.

"I'd l-like to run for p-president, p-p-please."

Her face shows no pity. She simply says, "Name."

"Amy P-p-price."

"You can only hang three posters. The debate is on October 24th. Good luck! Blast off!"

This is weird but I'll take it.

Maybe middle school weirdos end up being pretty cool adults.

CHAPTER EIGHT
Run Away

The next two weeks of school pass quickly. Each morning, I walk, rather than run, to P.S. 71.

Each day, I *proudly* eat lunch at the Weirdo Table. I loudly sing songs with Eli. By week two, I can sing the entire opening number to the Broadway musical *Hamilton* without fear. It is awesome.

On the third week of school, I am late because I had to carry my three posters on the subway. I roll them up in my locker. Digby's posters are already up. They all have pictures of desserts on them. I think his platform is based around junk food.

I sprint to Science. But, I am not quiet this time.

"Slow down, speedy!" Ms. Shelby calls out.

"Who are you? Usain Bolt?" she teases.

"Y-y-you know who Usain B-b-bolt is?"

"Of course! I'm the track coach here. You didn't know that? My runners listen to his playlist during warm-ups."

"I did, did, did not know that," I stammer.

"You look pretty fast. You should come to practice!"

"Th-thank you, but no. I'm r-r-running for pres-pres-president."

She makes a confused face. "Oh. Well, *I* didn't know that."

She smiles, but there is something sad about

the smile. She feels bad for me. Pity. I know pity when I see it. And, I hate pity. I hate when anyone pities me because I have a disability.

I quickly find my seat next to Jayden. He nods his head at me. Jayden is definitely tough. I was scared of him at first. But, I think there is something about him that is kind.

Ms. Shelby claps her hands. "Today: ocean debates!" She smiles.

I sweat.

"Debates are important in science. They are not arguments," Ms. Shelby says. She pauses. "They are public conversations."

She hands out slips of paper with our debate topics.

Mine says: "Ocean Conservation. Argue why we should conserve oceans. "

Ms. Shelby sets a timer for twenty minutes. I am supposed to brainstorm three debate points.

After twenty minutes, Ms. Shelby flicks the

lights off, then on.

"We will spend the last ten minutes of class practicing."

She claps her hands and says, "Oceans!"

Then she looks at Jayden and me. "Jayden and Amy. Argue your points. Jayden goes first."

Jayden calmly walks to the front of the room. He still looks angry. But he doesn't look nervous.

I walk to the front of the room. My legs shake. My hands are sweaty. They stick to the paper. My heart pumps.

My brain says, *Run! Now! Leave all of this behind! There is a better world out there! And it's in the fountain's drain!*

I push away this thought.

Jayden stands in front of the whiteboard. He argues his first point. Jayden speaks slowly. With a beat. Almost like a beat poet.

His voice is clear. Like a beat poet lawyer.

Jayden uses his angry vibe to convince us that we should not conserve the oceans. "Conservation costs money!" he says. "And we could be using that money for schools or technology. The ocean can take care of itself."

Jayden makes eye contact with the class. His speech is smooth. Like jazz.

Everyone claps.

I was not aware people might clap.

Jayden doesn't smile. He just nods and sits down.

Ms. Shelby says, "Well done, Jayden. Amy, your turn."

I look at the sea of students staring at me. The paper in my hand is soaked with my sweat. I try to clear my throat. But my brain is yelling, *RUN*!

My mind has too many thoughts. I stutter and stammer, "O-o-oceans are v-v-vital to our entire p-p-planet. We cannot, cannot, cannot…"

"Spit it out, girl!" someone yells.

Digby laughs really loudly and says, "Grammy Weirdo is the worst!"

The class breaks into laughter.

"Hey!" Ms. Shelby turns off the lights. "Everybody freeze!"

When the lights come on, I am gone.

I have left the room.

I am running away.

CHAPTER NINE
Dreams Down the Drain

I am back at the drain. My first-day drain.

I curl up in the dark space. My hands shake.

Who yells at someone who stutters? How wrong that speech pathologist was! People are not kind. They are terrible.

Yes, Mosaic kids were weirdos, but they were kind. ALWAYS.

And I am kind.

When I see someone is not good at running, I don't yell, "Hey loser! You are the worst!"

No. I don't say that. Saying that would make

me a bully!

You know what I do? I run a second lap with the slowest runners. I don't make fun of them at all. I just run there, with them, at their pace. Whatever that pace is. Because I learned the word "compassionate."

Maybe all Mosaic kids were brightly colored fish, but they were compassionate. They weren't predator panthers. That's for sure!

I'm going to leave. I'm going to buy a scuba suit and go underwater. Find a school of angelfish. Fish like Eli. Fish that are good. And polite. And kind. And funny.

I look for Eli's red Jordans, but I don't see them like on the first day. I listen for singing, but I don't hear any.

So, I text him, "AMY ALERT. EMERGENCY. MY LIFE HAS GONE DOWN THE DRAIN. ALSO, I AM IN THE DRAIN."

Within four minutes, I see my *not*-annoying

friend. Eli Michaels. With his awesome red Jordans.

When I see them, I climb out. He helps me out. Eli is holding the large yellow hula-hoop that is the bathroom pass.

"Isn't this a cool hoop?" He smiles. He swings the hoop around his waist. "I never have to pee. I just like getting this and hula-hooping for about half an hour. "

"Half an hour!" I laugh. "Does anyone ever c-c-ome looking for you?"

"Sometimes!"

Already Eli has done his work as a friend. He tells me to stand up and hop inside the hoop. I do. We are squished, but Eli smells really good, like strawberry shampoo.

"Amy Price for President!" he sings while hula-hooping.

I shake my head. I sing, "NOT president! Gonna live out here forever! Ever and ever!

Despite the weather."

Then he sings back in a high voice, "No, you're not."

And I sing in a low voice, "Yes, I am."

"No, you're not."

"Totally am!'

"Why?"

"Because I'm horrible at public speaking." Then I sing, "None of these suckers will vote for me! Because…they are awful human beings!" Since I am going to create a new life out here, I no longer need this school to like me.

Suddenly, Eli drops the hoop and stops singing. "That's it!" he says in a serious voice.

"What?" I reply.

"You should *sing* your speech!"

"No way. That will totally not work." I look at the drain. "Is that even allowed?"

"It will totally work, Amy Price," Eli says loudly. "You saw his posters. Digby's speech is just going to be about desserts. You can sing about something much more important!"

He starts singing so loudly that a teacher calls out from a window, "Get back to class, lovebirds!"

We blush. We are just good friends. *Not* in love. Eli picks up the hoop. We walk inside.

By the end of the day, I agree with Eli. I am going to sing my speech tomorrow.

CHAPTER TEN
Prepare to Lose

I am standing behind a podium. I look out at the auditorium of P.S. 71. I look at the huge crowd.

My glass of water shakes. Digby is to my left. The panther with his scorpion fish stinger. He clears his throat. He adjusts his bow tie. Then he looks at me, through the white lights of the stage. He smiles in a way that says, "Prepare to lose."

I try to smile back, but it's difficult to smile when you might puke.

The debate announcer is Digby's friend who I saw on the first day.

She introduces Digby as a "fearless leader." She says, "We all know when Digby is around because everyone is laughing!" She smiles sweetly at him. He winks at her. She winks back. If the school tells me I can't sing my speech, I'll say announcers can't flirt with candidates. Because they are *totally* flirting.

The announcer introduces me as "Amy Prince, a new student at the school who we don't really know."

"Amy P-p-price," I say.

"What?" she says. "Are you like an old-school CD, skipping?"

The auditorium laughs.

I shake my head, no.

Digby speaks first. His speech is all about desserts in the cafeteria.

"We should have more desserts," he says, "because they're fun! If you make me president, I'll put more desserts in the cafeteria. I'll give the students what they want! Because I know what you guys want. I get it. I know what's cool. And I know what's totally weird." When he says this, he looks straight at me.

"If you vote for the weirdo, who knows what she'll do? Vote for me. Digby!" He ends his speech by getting everyone to chant his name. Two hundred kids are shouting, "Digby! Digby!"

The announcer beams at him. She's in love. Great. "Wow! Excellent speech!"

"Your turn, P-p-p-rince," she says, under her breath.

I touch my left hand to my left ear. This signals Eli, who is backstage with an iPod and speaker. He hits play and gives me a nice steady beat. The audience looks up, confused.

I clear my throat. Clear my head. I am not a small girl. I am not my disability. I am not my stutter. I am DJ Price Is Right Bolt. And here I go:

"C-cookies are nice,
there's no denyin'.
But fried food, white sugar,
you gotta be lyin'.

That food is junk.
It slows us down,
keeps us down,
makes us clowns.
We gotta run to the beat
of what's around.

And that's yogurt, tofu,
spinach, tomatoes,
brown rice, applesauce,
and sweet potatoes.
If you elect Digby
your brain is bananas.
He bullies people who
dress like their grandmas.

All Digby can do is
bully and hate.
And I'm the way better
candidate.

I'm smart and I'm kind
and my stutter is cool.
I won't let you down—
I'll work for our school.

The price is right
when we all act nice.
So check my name
on your ballot:
AMY PRICE!"

And then I drop the mic. Actually drop it. Like a rapper. Except with shaky hands.

I scramble off the stage.

And then, I hear the crowd go wild.

CHAPTER ELEVEN
I Am a Weirdo

And so, on a rainy day in early November, on the cement steps of P.S. 71, I am sworn in. The principal gives me a uniform with the words "Panther President" written on the shirt. The letters are in gold. I put my hand on a book called *Public School 71: Rules for Respect* and take the oath.

The principal shakes my hand. She says, "I look forward to working with you, Ms. Price."

I chose Jayden as my vice president. He's serious and quiet. He's a good listener. He's also a better speaker than I am. If I need his help, he'll be there for me.

Eli sings the national anthem. He sings it so well. My eyes cry tiny tears of pride.

I look out at the students of P.S. 71. Their hair flies wildly in the wind. They smile at me. Their eyes are bright with respect.

I am a weirdo. An outsider. Someone unique and different. And I am exactly the kind of person for this job.

Want to Keep Reading?

Turn the page for a sneak peek at
the next book in the series.

ISBN: 9781538382059

CHAPTER ONE
Detention

My hoodie feels good. Warm. Like blankets.

And, it's gray. My favorite color.

I am at Public School 71. It is 3:17 p.m.

I'm in detention. Again. Always.

The teachers here don't understand me. No one does. I don't have any friends. Not one single friend. But, I don't want any.

I am quiet. Really quiet. I like listening better than talking. I don't know why everyone has to speak so loudly. All the time.

The kids here are yelling. They are loud. They call me names that are not my name.

My name is Jayden Jackson.

Not Jay-dawg.

Not Jay-son.

Not Jay-bird.

Jayden. Jackson.

The only people who can call me "Jay" are people I love. And that is five people: my mom, my dad, my sister Kiera, my sister Zion, and my dad's friend, Maurice. He's like a second dad.

These are the only cats who can call me Jay. When the P.S. 71 kids call me one of those other names, I explode.

Like a bomb. Like a firecracker. Like a bull.

I yell. Really loud. "THAT IS NOT MY NAME!"

Then, I get detention.

The only good part of detention is that it has a computer. And I've got headphones. Maurice gave them to me. Well, I bought them from him. But the price was so low, he pretty much gave them to me. He's a musician. So, he understands the need to hear music. All the time.

Right now, I'm listening to the band Animal Father. It's heavy metal.

I don't look like I would like heavy metal. But I do. It can go from quiet to angry in one second. I love it. Animal Father is all about control. I put my hoodie up. I sink into the music.

ABOUT THE AUTHOR

Charley Pickle holds
an MFA and is a published
poet and short fiction author.
In sixth grade, Pickle wore a historically
accurate Shakespeare costume to school on
Halloween. Sadly, no one else dressed up.
Feeling rather pathetic, Pickle quickly changed
into inspirational Shaquille O'Neal gym clothes.
Charley Pickle definitely knows what it's like
to be a weirdo and often seeks weirdo friends,
as they usually have tremendously good
senses of humor. Pickle can
be found on Twitter at
@charley_pickle.

WE THE
WEIRDOS

WE THE
WEIRDOS
Amy Price
FOR PRESIDENT!
VOTE
CHARLEY PICKLE

WE THE
WEIRDOS
ELI MICHAELS
RULE BREAKER
CHARLEY PICKLE

WE THE
WEIRDOS
WHAT'S THE MATTER WITH
JAYDEN JACKSON?
CHARLEY PICKLE

WE THE
WEIRDOS
MAKES HER MARK
CHARLEY PICKLE